★ CONTENTS ★

Who Lives in the Little House?

Who Stole Hare's House?

Who Lives in the Little House?

One day a box fell off a farmer's cart and rolled to the side of the road. A little frisky mouse came running by. What a perfect place to live, she thought.

She called out, "Little house!
Little house! Who lives in the little
house?" But there was no answer,
because no one lived there.

"Then I shall live in the little house all by myself," said Little Frisky Mouse. So she did, and very happy she was too.

Soon after that a flippity-floppity frog came along. He saw the little house and thought what a very nice house it was.

"Little house! Little house!
Who lives in the little house?"
croaked Flippity-Floppity Frog.

"I do," squeaked Little Frisky
Mouse. "I live in the little house.
But you can come in and live
with me."

So that's what he did. *Flip-flop-hoppity-hop* into the little house.

Little Frisky Mouse and Flippity-Floppity Frog lived together very happily.

Next a hoppity-skippity rabbit
came running by and saw the
little house.

"Little house! Little house!
Who lives in the little house?"
called Hoppity-Skippity Rabbit.

Little Frisky Mouse popped her head out. "I do," she squeaked.

"And I do," croaked Flippity-Floppity Frog. "But you can come in and live with us."

So Hoppity-Skippity Rabbit
hopped inside and lived in the
little house with them. And very
cosy it was too.

Another day a whiffly-whuffly
dog came snuffling down the road
and saw the little house.

"Little house! Little house! Who
lives in the little house?" he barked.

"I do," squeaked Little Frisky Mouse.

"And I do," croaked Flippity-Floppity Frog.

"And I do," said Hoppity-Skippity Rabbit.

"But you can come in and live with us," they told the dog.

So Whiffly-Whuffly Dog jumped inside and the four of them lived happily together. But it was a bit of a squeeze.

By and by a knobbly-gobbly
goat came trotting down the road.
He was looking for something to
eat but he found the little house
instead.

"Little house! Little house!
Who lives in the little house?"
cried Knobbly-Gobbly Goat.

"I do," squeaked
Little Frisky Mouse.

"And I do,"
croaked Flippity-
Floppity Frog.

"And I do,"
said Hoppity-
Skippity Rabbit.

22

"And I do," barked Whiffly-
Whuffly Dog.

"But you can come in and live
with us," they told the goat.

Now it was even more of a
squeeze in the little house, but
nobody minded.

Then one day a rumbling-
bumbling bear came out of the
woods. The ground shook and the
little house rocked.

"What have we here?" rumbled the bear. Then he said in a huge roaring voice, "LITTLE HOUSE! LITTLE HOUSE! WHO LIVES IN THE LITTLE HOUSE?"

All the animals peeped out of
the windows and said:
"Little Frisky Mouse
and Flippity-Floppity Frog
and Hoppity-Skippity Rabbit
and Whiffly-Whuffly Dog
and Knobbly-Gobbly Goat.
We all live in the little house.
Who are you?"

"I'M RUMBLING-BUMBLING BEAR
AND YOU'D BETTER LET ME IN THERE
'COS I'M BIG AND I'M FAT
AND I'LL SQUASH-YOU-ALL-FLAT."

"But there isn't any room,"
cried the animals. "Please don't
squash us flat."

Do you think that Rumbling-
Bumbling Bear took any notice?
No, he did not.

First he lifted his paw and Little
Frisky Mouse flew out of the door.

Then down his paw came
on top of the box and out flew
the lot: Flippity-Floppity Frog,
Hoppity-Skippity Rabbit,
Whiffly-Whuffly Dog and
Knobbly-Gobbly Goat. Just in
time before their house fell down.

Biff! Bang! Splat!
He squashed the house flat.
And that was that!

★ Who Stole Hare's House? ★

There was once a hare who went out for a walk and left his house open. A caterpillar came along and saw the house open and crawled inside.

When Hare came home he could see marks all around his door, so he knew someone had been there.

"Who is in my house?" he cried.

"A very fierce creature,"
Caterpillar called back. "I can
squash elephants."

When Hare heard this he
shivered and he shook. A creature
that can squash elephants can
easily scare a hare, he thought.

Hare didn't know what to do.
He walked up and down outside
his little house, muttering to himself,
"Oh dear, oh dear. Oh deary,
deary me."

Along the road came his friend Fox.

"My dear friend, Fox. Please talk to the fierce creature who has stolen my house."

"Leave it to me," said Fox. "I'm a rather fierce creature myself."

Fox called out
in a stern voice,
"Who is in
Hare's house?"

"*A very fierce
creature,*" shouted
Caterpillar.
"*I can squash
elephants.*"

Fox didn't like the sound of that.
A creature who could squash an
elephant could easily fight a fox,
he thought.

"I'm sorry," he told Hare. "I just
remembered something I have to do."

And Fox raced off down the road
leaving Hare pacing up and down,
muttering to himself, "Oh dear,
oh dear. Oh deary, deary me."

Next, Hare saw his friend Tiger coming towards him. "My dear friend, Tiger, thank goodness you have come. Please drive out the fierce creature who has stolen my house."

"No trouble at all," said Tiger.
"He'll listen to a tiger. You'll see."

Tiger puffed himself up and roared in a loud voice, "Now, then. Who is in the house of my friend, Hare?"

Caterpillar called back in an
even louder voice, *"A very fierce
creature. I can squash elephants."*

This made Tiger tremble.
A creature who could squash an
elephant could easily tie up a tiger.

"I'm sorry," he told Hare.
"I'm no match for such a fierce
creature." And Tiger ran away
with his tail between his legs.

Hare was shaking by now.
"Oh dear," he sighed. "Oh deary,
deary me."

Next, his friend Elephant came plodding along the road. Hare ran to meet him. He begged Elephant to come and get rid of the fierce creature who had stolen his house.

"Nothing could be easier,"
said Elephant. "Lead the way."

When Elephant reached Hare's house he bellowed, "Who is in the house of my good friend, Hare?"

But Caterpillar bellowed back, *"A very fierce creature. I can squash elephants."*

"Squash elephants?" said
Elephant. "Hmmm." And he
began to shake.

"Yes, and roll them flat like pastry,"
yelled Caterpillar.

Elephant didn't want to be rolled flat like pastry. He hurried off down the road and left Hare to sort out his own problem.

Just then a frog came by. Frog stopped and asked Hare what was wrong. So Hare told Frog about the very fierce creature who had stolen his house.

"Perhaps I can help," said Frog. And he went right up to Hare's house and croaked, "Who is in Hare's house?"

"*A very fierce creature,*" shouted Caterpillar in his very fiercest voice. "*I can squash elephants.*"

Now, you might think that a creature who could squash an elephant could easily frighten a frog. But this frog wasn't frightened. He opened the door and hopped inside.

He croaked in his loudest voice,
"Well, I'm a big strong frog and
I can jump and hop and squash
you flat."

Oh dear! Suddenly, Caterpillar didn't feel so brave. He said in a much smaller voice, "I'm really only a little c-c-caterpillar and I d-d-didn't mean any h-h-harm."

"Then off you go before I eat you up," said Frog.

And before he could, Caterpillar crawled out of the back door and raced down the road. And you can be sure he never came back.

Then Hare and Frog sat down
in Hare's house and drank tea
and ate cakes and told each other
stories all evening.

Caterpillar talked big.
But he wasn't so tough.
When Frog came along
And called his bluff.

There are many stories about different animals living together. *Who Lives in the Little House?* is a Russian folk tale, sometimes called *Who Lives in the Skull?* The story *Who Stole Hare's House?* comes from Africa.

Here are some more stories you might like to read:

About Animals Living Together:

The Cock, The Mouse and The Little Red Hen
from *The Orchard Book of Nursery Stories*
by Sophie Windham
(Orchard Books)

Little Cock, Feather Frock
from *The Singing Sack*
by Helen East
(A&C Black)

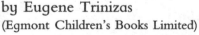

About Uninvited Visitors:

Three Little Wolves and the Big Bad Pig
by Eugene Trinizas
(Egmont Children's Books Limited)